Written for Middle and High School Students
and Their Parents

HELP YOUR KIDS
GET BETTER GRADES

A unique new grade-improvement book . . .
simple, enjoyable, easy-to-understand and implement,
it covers critical learning, studying and testing skills
rarely taught in U.S. schools and colleges.

by Gary E. Howard

Help Your Kits Get Better Grades
Copyright 2010 © Gary E. Howard

This book is designed to provide accurate and authoritative information with regard to the subject matter covered. It is sold with the understanding that the publisher is not engaged in rendering legal, accounting or other professional service. If legal advice or other expert assistance is required, the services of a competent professional person should be sought. (From a Declaration of Principles Jointly Adopted by a Committee of the American Bar Association and a Committee of Publishers and Associations.)

Graphic Design by Patty Floyd
Type & Image

First printing: June 2010

Printed in the United States of America

ISBN 978-0-9802091-1-2

DEDICATION

*This book is dedicated to those who know in their hearts that
they can become successful students, but lack the basic knowledge
of how to do it. Hopefully this book will provide that knowledge.*

This book is also dedicated to four special women:

*Mrs. Susan Sperry, my co-presenter of the
Cambridge Learning Skills Seminars,
who gave me permission to use her wonderful material on testing*

*Miss Carolina Quijano for her computer work
with the original text printing*

Mrs. Patty Floyd for her fantastic work with graphic design

*Mrs. Judie Howard, my wife, for supporting me
throughout the writing of this book and
for the super job she did editing the final manuscript*

ACKNOWLEDGEMENTS

*I would like to thank the following people for
providing critiques of this book:*

*Mr. Thomas Allen
Mr. Thomas Fryer
Mr. Paul Harris
Mr. Scott Howard
Mrs. Anmarie Medin*

TABLE OF CONTENTS

Introduction

This short, unique new grade-improvement book is specifically written for both parents and their students in middle and high school. Parents should read it first (it only takes an hour or two) and then have the student read it in a number of sessions. There are two reasons for this: One is that there are strategies and methods in it that may require parental help and support. The other is the fact that young students today are so overburdened with reading homework they are turned off by having to read anything else, much less a grade-improvement book, no matter how short and well-written it is. There are forty-seven subject-oriented short sections in this book. It is suggested that you have your student read twelve of them at a time, and then meet with you to go over the material covered.

After the final review session, your student should have a firm understanding of the main topics covered in this book, but will probably need some parental help and guidance implementing them. Making a major change in the way you have been addressing your education up until now is not an easy thing to do. The keys are to set up a well-equipped study place, establish a workable daily study schedule, adopt a simple note-taking system, determine what is the best learning style for you, improve your reading speed and comprehension, and learn the best strategies for studying for and taking tests. This all sounds overwhelming, but if it is done in small learning sessions, it is easily accomplished, especially while getting full parental support.

Adopting a simple-to-use and follow note-taking system is by far the most important of all these. The reason is that it is almost impossible to learn, study and prepare to take tests without such a system, as you will learn later in this book.

You will notice that the book is written all in the first person so that readers get the feeling that a close friend or relative is coaching them, unlike reading a typical grade-improvement text.

The book is also printed in easy-to-read and understand spaced-out type. There are forty-seven short sections that provide for easy learning and implementing. In short, this book was designed specifically for young readers who are easily distracted.

Almost every adult that has read this book has asked "Where was this book when I was back in school? If I had had a copy and had paid attention to it, I would have done much better in school and in my career."

This book was not written to be an extensive review of education in general. It was written to give the reader a basic understanding of the critical learning, studying and testing skills needed in order to become a successful student. These three skills are rarely taught in U.S. schools but have been an integral part of the British educational system for over three hundred years.

Almost every one of the industrialized nations in the world follows the British system of education. That system stresses teaching students the three critical academic skills from an early age. The U.S. does not. Perhaps this is one of the main reasons U.S. students do not compare favorably in test scores with students from these other countries. This book explains in detail these three critical academic skills.

It is the author's hope that this book will start a parental movement in the U.S. to incorporate teaching these three critical academic skills in all levels of education.

ENJOY, LEARN AND CHANGE

Gary E. Howard

1
U.S. High Schools Today

According to a recent analysis by the Education Department at John Hopkins University, nationally, only 70% of students starting high school will actually graduate. More than 10% of our nation's high schools – 1,700 to be exact – are dubbed "dropout factories" in which the dropout rate is 40%. With global competition increasing dramatically, America needs, like never before, an educated, trainable workforce. This soaring dropout rate means that a growing number of American young people will not be able to obtain well-paying jobs that will allow them to live "The American Dream." The No Child Left Behind Act, with its heavy emphasis on competency testing, will increase the number of students who DROP OUT. Some schools are trying innovative ways to try to stem this dropout rate, but on the whole not enough is being done.

IT IS MY HOPE THAT THIS BOOK WILL HELP YOU DEVELOP THE TALENTS YOU WERE BORN WITH.

2
Education Is Like A Game

Before we really get into the meat of this material, you need to know how to play this game called EDUCATION. You're saying to yourself, "What is this guy doing calling education a game?" Believe it or not, education is very similar to almost any game you play. Many games are played with some sort of ball: baseball, football, volleyball, basketball, soccer, tennis, golf, etc. You get the idea. In each of these games, you have to know and play by the rules or you get penalized. Education is the same. When learning how to play any of these games, you have to coach yourself, or be coached. Same thing applies to education. You also have to practice in order to learn how to throw the ball, hit the ball, catch the ball, etc. It is the same in education. You have to practice, only in education we call practice STUDYING.

Let's take just one of these sports, say baseball. You start out learning with your friends or parent teaching you the very basics. Once you have them learned, you advance to Little League ball. From there you advance to Junior League ball, then to high school ball, then to college ball, then to Minor League ball and finally, if you are really good and have learned to perform at the very best in the sport, you make it to the Pros. How many tens of thousands of hours do you think one of these athletes has to complete in order to reach this level? Best guess: tens of thousands of hours of practice individually, as well as working with a team.

EDUCATION IS THE EXACT SAME STORY. IF YOU WANT TO BE SUCCESSFUL IN THE PROFESSION YOU EVENTUALLY CHOOSE AND ENJOY THE EMOTIONAL AND FINANCIAL REWARDS THIS BRINGS, YOU WILL HAVE TO PAY YOUR DUES AND PRACTICE. REMEMBER, YOUR PRACTICE IS SPELLED S-T-U-D-Y-I-N-G.

3
Education Is Like A Job

It makes no difference what kind of job you have in this life, each one has its own set of tools, skills and procedures. The simple job of flipping burgers at a fast food restaurant requires some knowledge of basic cooking tools plus certain skills and procedures. Carpenters, plumbers and electricians must master the use of dozens of tools and have the skills to follow and understand involved blueprints or schematics, or they could not build, plumb or wire a house. All skilled tradespeople have to spend thousands of hours learning and practicing their trades in order to become successful at them. Can you possibly imagine dentists or surgeons doing their job without having spent thousands and thousands of hours studying and practicing before even touching a patient? One wrong slip and they could severely injure or kill someone.

Education is the same. In order for you to become successful and achieve good grades that will allow you to go on for a college education or advanced training of some sort, you have to pay your dues and put in thousands of hours of practice. In education we call practice STUDYING.

4
Money

I know what you're thinking: "Why is this guy now writing about money? Isn't this book supposed to be about learning and studying?" Yes it is, but hopefully you still have a long life to lead, and learning and money go together. How so? It is a simple fact that the more education you have, the higher level of employment you can obtain, which normally means the more money you can earn.

You are going to have to work approximately fifty years of your life at doing something. That's FIFTY as in THE BIG FIVE-0, so you want to make sure you are doing this work in a job that is safe, clean, interesting and pays you well enough to live "The American Dream." This is defined as having a nice home, car and standard of living that allows you to raise a family comfortably and then retire. What kind of income will you need to accomplish this? Current estimates are that you will have to have a family income of around $80,000 per year in today's dollars in order to do it. If you are the sole wage earner in the family this means that you will have to earn about $40 per hour. Currently construction workers earn about $25 per hour and office workers about $20 per hour.

Not all motivation is geared around money. Some students aspire to leadership roles in society. For others, the opportunity to do creative work in the arts, sciences and engineering will be their primary motivation. Some are motivated by altruism and want to help their fellow human beings. For all of these and more, financial rewards are of secondary importance.

No matter what your motivations are, you will need to do well academically in order to succeed. The information you will get from this short book will help you achieve your goals.

Unless you have some sort of advanced training (not necessarily a college degree) that separates you from the majority of workers, you will not even come close to living "The American Dream."

INCOMES BASED ON LEVEL OF EDUCATION
Based on 2006 Statistics

	Men	Women
Less than 9th grade.	$22,710	$18,130
9th to 12th (no completion)	$27,650	$20,130
High School completion.	$37,030	$26,740
Some college.	$43,830	$31,950
Associate Degree	$47,070	$35,160
Bachelor's Degree	$60,910	$45,410
Master's Degree.	$75,430	$52,440
Professional.	$100,000	$76,240

So what does this all mean in relation to LEARNING? It means that you are going to have to obtain some higher level of training after high school if you are going to enjoy success in life. You are going to have to become your own best teacher, not only for the time you are learning your new profession, but for the rest of your life in order to just keep up.

YOU ARE THE ONLY PERSON ON THIS PLANET THAT CAN MAKE THAT COMMITMENT.

Anyone with average intelligence can learn and understand the material presented here. Your challenge will be to adopt these methods and strategies so that they become a habit you will stick with.

5
Poor Grades Are Not All Your Fault

You are not solely to blame for earning poor grades. A good part of the blame goes to our current educational system in the United States. Students are not born knowing how to get organized, learn, study, prepare to take tests and take tests. Some are lucky enough to have parents or relatives or friends or teachers who teach them these skills. But the vast majority of students stumble along in grade school and high school not knowing that they should be following a specific learning plan best suited to their personality. No one has clued them in to the many educational learning methods that will aid them in their studies.

I personally believe that every student in the U.S. should be given a short course that covers these skills and methods as early as intermediate school and repeated if necessary at the high school level. It is my hope that this book will in some way encourage schools and colleges to adopt and offer such a course for their students.

6
Plan Or No-Plan Prior To Entering High School

The vast majority of students entering high school today do not have any sort of plan in mind before taking on the forty courses contained in the average high school program. Why should they? They have not been taught that without a specific plan of attack they are doomed to doing poorly in those forty courses. Some are lucky enough to have had a family member or friend clue them in as to what they have to do, but most just stumble along and try to do their best. This path will lead to possible graduation, but with grades so low that they will never qualify for college or some other type of advanced training.

Almost every expert on this topic has stated that in order to become a successful student in high school and graduate with B and A grades, you must have a workable plan. They further state that this plan must include learning, studying and testing skills. Each of these skills, and more, are covered in this book.

Like any plan, it looks difficult to accomplish at first. But, after taking it step-by-step and sticking to it, it becomes much easier, so much easier that your study time is reduced. So you have time for fun activites and, most important of all, you gain a feeling of control over your academic life.

This control also gives you a feeling of self-worth. The anxieties you had with studying, learning and testing might not totally disappear, but they are reduced to a point that they are a non-factor. This makes you a happy, successful student whose parents are thrilled by the change in you. This in turn earns you some much-wanted and needed perks, so it is a win-win situation for all concerned.

7

Your High School Transcript

PROBABLY THE MOST IMPORTANT DOCUMENT IN YOUR LIFE

I realize that is quite a statement, so let me back it up. You get one chance (only one) to earn excellent grades in the forty courses that make up the typical high school curriculum. These forty course grades are listed on your high school transcript, and it is this transcript that is your ticket to higher education or some other sort of advanced training.

If the sum total of these forty courses do not add up to a respectable grade point average, you will have a very difficult time entering the college of your choice. In short, your chances of experiencing "The American Dream" of a well-paying, secure profession and a happy, successful life are slim at best. The table on page 12 will show you fairly accurately the income you can expect depending on the level of education you finally reach. Many students do not come to this realization until it is too late to make a change in their learning, studying and testing habits. Don't become one of them.

You and only you control your destiny. Adopt most of the methods and strategies explained in this book and you will go a long way toward not becoming another high school graduate without the ability to advance yourself.

Sure, you can complete those missing courses at an adult school or a comminity college later, but likely you will be working full time and perhaps be raising a family. These responsibilities will make it very difficult for you to complete the four or five missing courses you <u>could</u> have and <u>should</u> have taken while in high school.

A section at the back of this book gives a detailed explanation and listing of courses for both the regular high school program and the college prep program. It is based on the requirements for California schools, but is somewhat universal in the U.S. There is also a planning form so that you and your parents, along with help from your school counselor, can decide which program is best suited to your abilities.

8
Your Study Places

Almost every single book you read on learning stresses the fact that students need a private study place of their own both off and on campus. On campus it is usually the library, if your school has one, or some quiet place where you can concentrate without being interrupted.

Off campus it is usually your home, so this means a suitable study area, probably in your bedroom. It does not have to be a fancy desk; a simple, sturdy fiberglass-topped, metal-legged 24"x 60" table will do fine. These can be purchased at Costco, Office Max or Staples for around $40. The really important piece of furniture you need to spend a lot of time selecting is your chair. You are going to spend thousands of hours here, so you had better make darn sure it is super-comfortable. Get a high-backed, heavily padded manager's chair with arms. Fairly good ones on sale can be bought for around $75. Don't skimp on this purchase; you just might be using it for four years of high school followed by four years of college. THAT'S A LOT OF SITTING.

If you are working with a very limited budget, you can go to your local Goodwill store or a second-hand furniture store and buy a used folding card table and chair. Most dollar stores sell pocket-book sized dictionaries and a thesaurus. When you can afford it, upgrade to the books and furniture listed in this book.

Besides a large work area and a comfortable chair, you will need a good work light and other various office supplies normally associated with a functional desk. The following is a listing of the minimum reference books you will need. The four following reference books and the encyclopedia CD-ROM I strongly recommend can be purchased from <u>Amazon.com</u> on the internet. The total for all five is currently less than $85. These are excellent reference books the entire family can use.

- *Merriam Webster Collegiate Dictionary*

- *Merriam Webster Collegiate Thesaurus*

- *New College World Atlas*

- *World Almanac and Book of Facts*

- *Compton's Interactive Encyclopedia for Windows CD-ROM*

You are not done organizing just yet. In addition, you will need a <u>large desk calendar</u> that shows the month at a glance. Office supply stores have them for around $5. You will also need two <u>2" thick, 3-ring binders</u> to keep your class and text notes in.

You will also need <u>several 8½"x 11" cheap wire spiral binders</u> that have 3-ring holes punched in each page. (More on these when we take up note-taking.)

<u>Flash Cards</u>: Buy a small pack of 3"x 5" index cards. You will use these to remember various lists of names, places, dates, etc. (More on flash card use later in the book.)

<u>Pocket Day-At-A-Glance Calendar</u>: You will need one of these in order to keep track of homework assignments, test dates, phone numbers and addresses. If you are fortunate enough to own a cell phone that has features to cover this information, use it.

9
The Right Pen

Now we come to the selection of what pen you are going to use. Most people give this decision very little thought and go with whatever they have available. THIS IS A BIG MISTAKE. You are going to be using this type of pen for thousands of hours, in class and in your study place. You need to select a pen that is right for you. This may seem silly to you at this point, but believe me, <u>the right pen makes all the difference when you need to take extensive notes or write long essay answers on an exam</u>. You need to try out different types of pens and see which one best meets your individual needs. Here are some considerations you might want to think about when selecting one:

1. Fine or medium point? Go with the fine, you will see why shortly.

2. Blue or black? Go with black or dark blue because they photocopy better.

3. Traditional ball point or the gel pens? Go with the gel pen; it has become the number one pen in the U.S. for a good reason. The ink just seems to flow off the tip

and makes writing a lot easier. I personally like the Pilot G-2 07. Most of these gel pens have a fatter diameter where your fingers grasp the pen. This makes it easier to hold, especially over long periods of writing.

I recommend the fine point because it is easier to print with a fine point pen rather than a medium point pen. (More on why I think you should consider printing rather than writing in the next few pages.)

10
Print Or Write

Unless your handwriting is very good and you can do it quickly, I strongly recommend you print all your notes in lower case letters. It takes dramatically fewer pen strokes to print in lower case letters than it takes to print in capital letters, thereby speeding up your note-taking. I have found that in the past thirty years more and more students are printing their notes, homework and tests instead of writing them. The reason for this is simple: most public schools spend little time teaching penmanship the way they used to, and students find it easier to print.

Another reason to print in small case letters is that you can take notes in and out of class that you can read easily, not having to rewrite them each night as most learning texts recommend.

It is far better to rewrite your notes each night after class because that doubles your note learning, but from experience I have found that most students do not do this.

From my personal experience with writing my notes

in and out of class, I found that when I was under pressure to take notes fast and to write fast in an exam situation, my handwriting went in the dumpster and became almost illegible to the point that even I could hardly read it. What do you think the teacher thought when grading my work?

Remember, you are now taking notes in wire spiral binders that are college ruled, so you do not have as much space as traditional ruled papers have. Finally, by printing neatly in lower case letters your work can be read by the teacher more easily, and therefore you stand a better chance of getting a higher grade. I know that a lot of you have printed very little in lower case letters before so I have provided printing samples on the following page for you to review.

Give this printing a real try, and I am sure that most of you will see the wisdom of adopting it. Once you do, you will find that you can print faster than you used to write.

ABBREVIATIONS
AND PRINTING SAMPLES

/	ratio, ratio of	&	and
%	percent, percentage	+	plus, positive
#	number	−	minus, negative
$	dollars	÷	divided (by)
¢	cents	X	times, multiplied by
( )	parenthetical	=	equals, is the same as
∧	insert, insertion	≠	doesn't equal
@	amount, the amount of, at		is not the same as
?	question, the question is	≅	is approximately equal to
!	here's a surprising fact		is similar
cf	compare	<	is less than
eg	for example		is increasing to
c/o	care of	>	is more than
lb	pound		is decreasing to
H_2O	water	→	approaches, approaching
min	minimum		to the end
max	maximum	V	varies, varying, varied
sub	subordinate	∠	angle
subj	subject	⊥	perpendicular
ca	approximately	‖	parallel
ng	no good	f	frequency, frequent(ly)
dept	department		
etc	and so forth		

11
Basic Computer Skills

I would be remiss if I did not at least provide a brief section on Computer Skills. Today, with computers available to everyone in one way or another, it is very important to list the absolute basic computer skills a student should have. I feel a student must have the following three: One is to be able to send and receive emails. The second is the ability to enter the internet and search for specific information. Finally, a student needs to be able to type up a report using a word processing program like Word.

These three computer skills are easily learned. All you need is a patient and knowledgeable friend to spend a few hours with you teaching you how to use them. There are many books available covering these, but I have found that having a friend help you with the hands-on learning is far better.

Deciding what computer to buy is a very personal decision. Ask yourself which kind would be best for you and can you afford it.

There are two basic types of computers: desktop or laptop. There are two basic operating systems: PC (Microsoft) or MAC (Apple). When it comes to desktop or laptop, you need to consider how you are going to use the computer. If it is going to stay at your desk all the time, then choose a desktop. If you really feel that you need it to be portable, then choose a laptop.

Desktops are far more powerful than most laptops and are usually tied to a printer and have a connection to the internet. Many students like the laptop because they can take it with them to school or college and work on it almost anywhere. Laptops have their limitations such as battery life, cost of portable internet service, the bother of having to wire it to a printer and the fact that good ones with a large screen and large memory are more costly than a desktop.

Since this is going to be your biggest investment prior to buying a car, I would seriously recommend that you go to the library and check out what *Consumer Reports* has to say about the latest computers.

12
You Remember…

As you can see from the chart below, the more senses included in your learning the better off you are.

Only **20%** of what you **READ**.

Only **30%** of what you **HEAR**.

Only **40%** of what you **SEE**.

Only **50%** of what you **SAY**.

Only **60%** of what you **DO**.

But you remember **90%** of what you learn using many sensory learning activities: **READ, HEAR, SEE, SAY, and DO**.

Visual Images

For many students, especially those visually-oriented ones, visual images are a great help. If they are included in your text, you can be sure they are important enough for you to study and copy or duplicate for your notes if possible.

13
Studying

The main way you are going to study is by daily reviewing your notes from lectures and readings, but there are some other things you need to understand about successful studying. The following should be very helpful.

When and How to Study

1. The first thing you absolutely have to do is set up a Weekly Study Schedule (shown on page 43). Your goal should be to schedule two forty-minute study times each day with a twenty-minute break between. Pick the times that would be best for you. The important thing here is to STICK TO THESE TIMES.

2. I know the first thing you're going to say is, "What if I have a date, or practice or some concert to go to?" Fine, you can keep the Study Schedule flexible, but you had better put an extra night's studying in the bank prior to the event in order to stay up with the schedule. Trying to make it up after the event just does not work. You'll note that this schedule allows you to schedule the must-do daily things including sleeping, eating,

going to class, etc. Obviously, you have to schedule your study time when these other activities are not scheduled.

3. Do not schedule a study session immediately after a meal. You will not be able to concentrate while your stomach is working. Trust me.

4. I have already gone over where you should study earlier.

5. "To Do" lists are great to use when scheduling tasks you have to complete. Use one list for things you have to do that day, and one list for tasks that are due that week. Start with the task that is due the earliest.

6. Do not procrastinate so that you have to rush through a task. You will end up doing a crummy job of it.

7. Do one task at a time.

8. When you have completed the task, put it in a binder in your backpack.

9. As I have said before, use black or dark blue ink and PRINT.

10. Place all due dates on your large desk calendar.

Study Guides

BRIEF SYNOPSIS, EASIER TO READ. QUICK AND EASY WAY TO GET OVERVIEW OF SUBJECT INFORMATION.

Study Guides have been around for a long, long time. They are available on line and at your local book store. They can cover over 450 different subjects, and are primarily for high school and college courses. They should be viewed as supplementary sources of information. In no way should they be considered as cheating. All you are doing is getting information on a given subject that has been reduced to a detailed outline form by professionals. They are wonderful for determining the outline of a course and listing the main topics covered. I only wish I had known about them earlier in my academic career.

If you want to know the key items on a subject and learn them in the shortest period of time, Study Guides are for you. These come anywhere from two to six pages long and are usually printed on plastic-covered paper. They cost anywhere from $5.00 to $9.95 plus tax and shipping if you order them on line. The major publisher for these guides is Quick Study, and they can be reached on line at Quickstudy.com.

At the start of every high school and college course, I strongly urge you to check out these guides to see if they will be of any help to you. Most academic course guides are stocked at major book stores. If nothing else, they will tell you exactly what the course is going to be about.

Study Groups

After you have learned the facts and ideas that have been covered in class and in your reading assignments, it is a good idea to form a study group with a few classmates that want to join such a group. Here are some of the benefits and things to be aware of:

1. Discussing ideas and facts covered in class will help you develop long term memory for the topic.

2. Do not just listen; become an active participant.

3. Ask one another questions and then discuss the answers.

4. Choose a place that is quiet and free of distractions.

5. Remember, this is supposed to be a study session, not a social gathering.

Tutoring

If you are anything like I was when I was young, you want nothing to do with a tutor because it would be embarrassing. Believe me those days are gone.

Do you think that every–and I mean every– top athlete, skilled worker or professional does it on his or her own? Absolutely not. They have tutors. They may go by different names: coach, trainer, consultant, adviser, etc., but by any other name they are still getting tutoring help, so why shouldn't you?

If you can get through a difficult topic you are trying to learn by seeing a trained tutor in that field, WHY NOT TAKE ADVANTAGE OF IT? Our oldest son, who has a very successful networking consulting business, pays over $5,000 to attend a 30-hour top-level training class covering new advanced networking software. Is he embarrassed to seek out the help of a TUTOR? No, because the knowledge he gains for the money spent will come back in higher future earnings.

Most schools have Tutorial Centers; they are usually free, so why not take advantage of them? If you are embarrassed that someone will see you, then hire a private tutor. Many schools and colleges list students willing to tutor in various subjects for reasonable rates. Craigslist.org is also a good source for finding tutors.

IT IS FOOLISH NOT TO SEEK HELP WHEN YOU WILL BENEFIT FROM IT.

14

Good Student Habits

The dictionary says a habit is "a thing done often and hence usually done easily; a pattern of action that is acquired and has become so automatic that it is hard to break."

Learning better study habits is not the easiest thing in the world to do, but you must do this if you want to be a successful student.

In this book we cover a large number of topics that require you to adopt as habits. You should make a habit of:

1. Keeping your study place organized.

2. Making a weekly study schedule and sticking to it. (See example on page 43.)

3. Making an effort to improve your reading skills.

4. Using the learning skills that are best for you.

5. <u>Taking good notes for lectures and readings</u>. (This is by far the most important habit.)

6. Maintaining your master 3-ring note binder.

7. Making up a master study list for all tests.

8. Remembering the different test strategies.

9. Using the Brain Drain prior to all tests.

10. Looking for help on web sites and study guides.

You are certainly not required to start a habit for each of the above topics at one time, but at least try to start some of them.

Remember what the dictionary says: "A habit is a thing done often and hence usually done easily." There is an old saying that I remember: "Many times you have to fail at something before you can do it successfully." Think of the things you have tried to do in life and have failed at, but after failing – several times – you became successful.

So, the moral of this is: Give the difficult academic things your best shot, and if you fail, you are then just that much closer to accomplishing it the second time you try. Remember that the best minds on this planet got there with lots of support and help from others.

WEEKLY STUDY SCHEDULE

HOURS		MONDAY	TUESDAY	WEDNESDAY	THURSDAY	FRIDAY	SATURDAY	SUNDAY
A.M.	12 - 5							
	5 - 6							
	6 - 7							
	7 - 8							
	8 - 9							
	9 - 10							
	10 - 11							
	11 - 12							
P.M.	12 - 1							
	1 - 2							
	2 - 3							
	3 - 4							
	4 - 5							
	5 - 6							
	6 - 7							
	7 - 8							
	8 - 9							
	9 - 10							
	10 - 11							
	11 - 12							

15
Backpacks

The use of backpacks started about 30-40 years ago because up until that time students were given wall lockers to use. These lockers became long-term storage for rotting fruit, moldy sandwiches and smelly athletic equipment. As the year progressed, the halls, then the entire school began to smell terrible.

Later, when drugs were introduced into the schools, the lockers became a storage place for dealing drugs. The schools finally decided to end the use of lockers and allow students to bring backpacks to school. Now we have a whole generation of students who have never known anything else.

Backpack use is now almost a requirement for con-scientious students, because they have to have some place to carry their books and supplies. Unfortunately, many students have gone overboard with this idea and are packing 25-30 pound packs, risking back injury. Here is a sensible list of what you should carry in your pack:

1. Wire bound 8½"x 11½" notebook

2. At least two fine-point pens

3. Two pencils

4. Only the texts or books needed for that day's work

5. Compass, ruler, hand-held calculator

6. A couple of small Kleenex packets, in case there is no toilet paper when you need it

7. Some energy bars in case you forget your lunch or need a snack

8. Any medications you need (Tums, Advil, etc.)

9. Personal hygiene items

10. Two dollars in change for lunch or phone calls

11. A lightweight windbreaker in case of wind, rain or cold

12. Any other lightweight item you need

All the small items should be put in one of those plastic bags that are meant to be snapped in a 3-ring binder, or in a one gallon baggie.

All of this should weigh less than 5-8 pounds, which is easy to carry.

**REMEMBER TO PRINT YOUR NAME,
ADDRESS AND PHONE NUMBER IN
INDELIBLE INK ON YOUR PACK
IN CASE IT GETS LEFT BEHIND OR LOST.**

This is going to be a long-term investment, so do not go cheap. Jansport has one of the best names in packs. Limit the size of your pack to no more than 1500cc. This is plenty big enough to carry all your school needs. Many stores have special sales on good backkpacks for reasonable prices prior to the start of the school year.

16
Reading

Without a doubt, reading is one of the major ways we learn. Unfortunately, most young people today read very little, so they have become poor readers. They get their information from TV, movies, the internet, CDs, DVDs, the radio and other sites. This is troubling to a lot of learning experts because it's only possible to learn so much from these sources. The in-depth learning that is required for most of our technical and professional occupations must be learned through reading. Good reading skills give you the opportunity to become your own best teacher. There is a great deal of difference between reading a novel for enjoyment and reading a text for content. While reading a novel, you can let your brain go into a relaxed mode and just go with the flow of the writing. In reading for content and learning, you have to constantly pay attention to what is being written and absorb as much of the information as you can.

Reading provides us with the ability to keep up-to-date on current local, national and international happenings found in the daily paper, weekly news magazine or the internet. Each of us needs to become an informed citizen in order to understand what is happening around us and in the world. How is it possible to vote intelligently unless you have read up on all the political, religious, environmental, social and economic happenings of the day?

Like it or not, reading is the main way schools and colleges are set up to help you learn, so you need good reading skills if you really wish to become a successful student. To have your reading skills in order, you need to know your reading speed. Obviously, a slow reader is going to have a much more difficult time learning than one who reads quickly. It has been determined that an entering freshman in college should have a reading speed of at least 300-325 WPM (words per minute) to be considered average. If you read at 400 WPM your rate is average for a college senior. If your rate is below 250 WPM you are an extremely slow reader, and you are in great need of learning to read more rapidly.

The following is a simple test you can take to determine roughly what your reading speed is. Read the passage on pages 52-54 at your normal rate, making sure that you time yourself to the second. On page 55 there is a table that shows where you stand with regard to your reading speed. I will cover improving your reading speed later on in this book. My wife has told our sons "When you have a good book to read, you always have a friend." I know from experience, after meeting with thousands of students over the years, that they are burned out on reading. They have to read so much for their classes that reading a novel for enjoyment just does not happen. I felt the same way until I discovered several authors that really turned me on to reading. They have the ability to place you in a time capsule and take you to destinations and events that you would never be able to experience by yourself. When reading their books, I find myself cheering for some one or some thing, actually crying for some sad situations and becoming so totally engrossed in adventures that I find myself shaking with fear or from joy. Go to the library and ask the librarian for book ideas based on your individual interests and gain a whole new experience in reading.

THE READING TEST

START

As far back as I can remember there have been complaints about the schools for not teaching the young to write and to speak well. The complaints have focused mainly on the products of high school and college. An elementary school diploma never was expected to certify great competence in these matters. But after four or eight more years of school, it seemed reasonable to hope for a disciplined ability to perform these basic acts. English courses were, and for the most part still are, a staple ingredient in the high school curriculum. Until recently, freshman English was a required course in every college. These courses were supposed to develop skill in writing the mother tongue. Though less emphasized than writing, the ability to speak clearly, if not with eloquence is also supposed to be one of the ends in view.

The complaints came from all sources. Businessmen, who certainly did not expect too much, protested the incompetence of the high school students who came their way after school. Newspaper editorials by the score echoed their protests and added a voice of their own, expressing the misery of the editor who had to blue-pencil the stuff college graduates passed across his desk.

$\rightarrow$

Teachers of freshman English in college have had to do over again what should have been completed in high school. Teachers of other college courses have complained about the impossibly sloppy and incoherent English which students hand in on term papers and examinations.

And anyone who has taught in graduate school or in a law school knows that a B.A. from our best colleges means very little with reference to a student's skill in writing or speaking. Many a candidate for the Ph.D. has to be coached in the writing of his dissertation, not from the point of view of scholarship or scientific merit but with respect to the minimum requirements of simple, clear, straightforward English. My colleagues in the law school frequently cannot tell whether a student does or does not know the law because of his inability to express himself coherently on a point in issue.

I have mentioned only writing and speaking, not reading. Until very recently, no one paid much attention to the even greater and more prevalent incompetence in reading, except perhaps, the law professors who, ever since the introduction of the case method of studying law, have realized that half the time in a law school must be spent in teaching the student how to read cases. They thought, however, that this burden rested peculiarly on them, that there was something very

$\rightarrow$

special about reading cases. They did not realize that if college graduates had a decent skill in reading, the more specialized technique of reading cases could be acquired in much less than half the time now spent.

One reason for the comparative neglect of reading and the stress on writing and speaking is a point I have already mentioned. Writing and speaking are, for most people so much more clearly activities than reading is. Since we associate skills with this activity, it is a natural consequence of this error to attribute defects in writing and speaking to lack of technique, and to suppose that failure in reading must be due to lack of industry rather than skill. The error is gradually being corrected. More and more attention is being paid to the problem of reading. I do not mean that the educators have yet discovered what to do about it, but they have finally realized the schools are failing just as badly, if not worse, in the matter of reading as in writing and speaking.

STOP

Reading Time	Words Per Minute
30 sec	1,222
41 sec	815
1 min	611
1 min 15 sec	490
1 min 30 sec	410
1 min 45 sec	350
2 min	305
2 min 15 sec	270
2 min 30 sec	245
2 min 45 sec	220
3 min	205
3 min 15 sec	190
3 min 30 sec	175
3 min 45 sec	163
4 min	153
4 min 15 sec	144
4 min 30 sec	136
4 min 45 sec	128
5 min	122

LENGTH OF SELECTION: 622 WORDS

This rate is not absolute, for your reading speed normally varies according to the difficulty of the material. But this figure is a good indication of your speed in reading simple, easily understood prose.

Once again, if your rate is below 250 WPM you are a slow reader. You are in great need of learning to read more rapidly.

For help to increase your reading speed, enter "Improve your reading speed" in your internet search engine and several excellent sites will be listed. Choose the one titled "Speed Reading Test Online" to double-check your speed. Check out the other sites to find one that would be best for you.

17
Ways To Improve Your Reading Speed

If you feel that you read too slowly for your grade level, here are some steps you can take to improve your reading speed.

▶ Make sure you have sufficient lighting in your reading area so you do not tire your eyes. Having inadequate lighting makes it difficult to read for longer periods of time.

▶ Make sure you have a comfortable reading area. Pay special attention to your chair and to the room temperature. If these two things are not satisfactory, you will tire easily and not be able to sit still long enough to read your assigned reading.

▶ Limit your distractions and put your full attention on your reading. The fewer distractions, the more likely you will be to complete your assignment.

▶ Practice, practice, practice! Like anything else, if you practice reading, that will help increase your reading speed. Whether you pick up a newspaper or a magazine, it will help improve your reading rate and help you deal with difficult texts. It will also help improve your vocabulary and your reading comprehension.

▶ Try to go into each reading assignment with an interested and open mind. This will help keep your focus on what you're reading.

▶ Avoid reading the words aloud, or reading words over and over again. Each of these slows your reading rate. If you are unable to read in a manner different from the above, perhaps a reading specialist is needed. The internet has a number of helpful sites covering this subject.

18
Reading Texts And Assigned Reading

This will probably be one of the most important sections of this book because most students have trouble reading for content, whether it be textbooks or assigned readings. The approach I am going to explain here is not new. It has been used by students for well over one hundred years in colleges and universities all over the world. It is the simplest and most straightforward way to comprehend (attack, if you will) a chapter in a textbook.

The first thing you have to recognize is that most chapters in textbooks are designed by their authors and the publishers to make it easy for you to learn from them. The reason is simple: If you can learn easily from a text, teachers will like it and re-order it, thereby increasing the sale of the book. So what do they do to make learning easier? The first thing they do is provide a comprehensive introduction to each chapter where they tell you in short terms what they are going to teach you. The second thing they do is make the body of the chapter as easy to understand as possible by doing any and all of the following:

1. Use **bold** type or *italicize* important words or phrases

2. Present the material in short paragraphs so you can better understand it

3. Give you as many diagrams, pictures, graphs and any other graphic they can to help you understand the information

4. Provide you with examples of the ideas that are being covered

5. Use color and drawings to make or highlight their points

6. Provide a conclusion paragraph at the end of the chapter that covers the important points covered in the chapter.

7. And finally, most provide a list of questions to be answered at the end of the chapter. You should really pay attention to these questions and do your best to answer them, even if it means going back and finding the answers in the chapter. Why? Because you stand an excellent chance of seeing them or ones just like them on a test used by the teacher.

With this information it is not difficult to have you understand how to read a text chapter.

1. The first thing you are going to do is skim-read the entire chapter, paying particular attention to the seven points I have outlined earlier. This should only take you five to ten minutes, depending on the size of the chapter, and will give you a good overview of what the chapter is going to try to teach you.

2. Next you are going to read the chapter very carefully for content, taking notes on the major points covered. I'm not talking about reading for reading's sake, <u>I mean your brain is on full alert and you are paying full attention to what you are reading</u>. If you find yourself reading a paragraph or page and then not remembering what it contained, STOP right there and go back and read it with your brain in gear.

In other words . . . CUT OUT THE DAYDREAMING WHILE READING TEXTBOOKS.

If you have trouble taking notes while reading a text, please do not underline or highlight important sections. That just about makes the text worthless when it comes time to trade it in for a new text next semester. You will also find that you end up underlining or highlighting nearly everything in the chapter. If you must mark important points as you read, and you own the book, do so with a light pencil check next to the section you want to remember. When you finish the chapter go back and make notes from the checked sections, then erase the check marks. This will keep your textbooks in like-new condition. When you go to the bookstore next semester to trade in the texts you do not want to keep, they will bring top dollar. With the very high costs of textbooks today, this is very important.

Now you have a planned approach to text reading, just like you are going to learn how to have a planned approach that will ensure academic success for a number of learning, studying and testing situations. Remember the old saying: "Plan your work and work your plan."

19
Basic Learning Styles

There are three major learning styles: Visual, Auditory and Kinesthetic. Experts vary in their opinions as to what percentage of the population each style uses, but the following percentages are close:

Visual	62%
Auditory	28%
Kinesthetic	10%

As you can see, Visual is the most predominant style and that is probably because there are so many visual modes available to visual learners and U.S. schools cater to this type of learner.

Which Learning Style is Best For You?

The following is a brief description of each of the three learning styles. Please remember that you do not have to follow one style. Many people, including this writer, adopted learning strategies from all three styles.

Visual Learning Style

As you can imagine, people who use this style depend heavily on what they see. Visually-oriented people like all kinds of visual aids: videos, television, books, graphs, charts, maps and movies.

Auditory Learning Style

Obviously, auditorily-oriented people do most of their learning by listening. They do well by listening to class lectures, audio tapes, discussion groups, music and anything that they can learn from by listening. They do well with oral presentations rather than written ones.

Kinesthetic Learning Style

If you are a hands-on type of learner, this is your style. Kinesthetically-oriented learners learn best by actually doing something that they can see and feel. They do well with tasks that get them involved figuring out how things work.

Why Know Your Learning Style?

There are many reasons to know what learning style is best for you. The following are a few of the ways to:

- Improve your self-esteem and self-confidence
- Get to the point where you enjoy learning
- Learn the best way to use your brain
- Reduce your classroom failures
- Help eliminate your stress and frustration
- Do better on tests and exams
- Learn about the strategies in each style
- Become an active learner and your own best teacher
- Get the most out of your own abilities

REMEMBER . . . YOU ARE NOT LIMITED TO ONE SINGLE LEARNING STYLE, SO UTILIZE THE ADVICE FROM ALL THE STYLES THAT MIGHT HELP YOU. MANY PEOPLE ARE A COMBINATION OF ALL THREE STYLES, EVEN THOUGH ONE MIGHT BE DOMINANT.

Characteristics of a Visual Learner

- Is a good speller
- Is detail-oriented
- Is well-organized and neat
- Likes all types of reading materials
- Likes any type of visual aid such as flashcards, graphs, notes, diagrams. etc.
- Has a good memory of sighted materials
- Needs an organized and quiet place to study
- Takes excellent notes and maintains them

Advice for Visual Learners

- Always sit in the front of the classroom
- Take excellent notes in class
- When studying, color-code major points on notes
- Write down everything the teacher writes on the chalkboard and accept all written teacher-made materials
- Watch instructional videos
- Use illustrations to help you remember key points
- Do everything you can to maximize your learning by utilizing visual means

Characteristics of an Auditory Learner

- Is helped by reading aloud
- Has an excellent memory
- Usually talks in class
- Likes oral reporting, not written reporting
- Enjoys music and talking to friends
- Likes debates and discussion groups
- Learns best through lectures, oral presentations and anything auditory
- Loves to sing
- Finds languages easy to learn
- Has difficulty with visual learning materials
- Is a slow reader
- Does well in study groups

Advice for Auditory Learners

- Read texts aloud when studying
- Take part in class discussions
- Use rhymes to remember dates, names, etc.
- When possible, use audio learning devices
- Watch and listen to instructional videos
- Ask questions in class
- Try your best to take class notes
- If you can, record and listen to taped lectures

Characteristics of a Kinesthetic Learner

- Good at mastering skills by actual participation
- Often good at musical instruments and dancing
- Not a strong speller or handwriter
- Loves to collect things
- Likes action-oriented activities
- Talks fast and often
- Never saw a demonstration s/he did not like
- Best at remembering by actually doing things
- Loves role playing
- Good at sports
- Is not distracted by auditory sounds
- Has a hard time studying for long periods
- Is a touchy-feely type of person

Advice for Kinesthetic Learners

- Use activity with body any time you can for learning
- Take advantage of educational field trips
- Practice a task until you learn it
- Study lying down on a sofa
- Write down notes when reading or studying
- Sit near the front of the class to avoid distractions
- When you can, make a model
- Use music to help you learn and remember things
- Whevever you can, use action and motion to help you learn

21
Why Proper
Note-Taking Is Critical

Just for a moment consider learning, studying and test preparation without the use of notes. In lectures you would be forced to try to remember all the important points covered. In reading texts and assigned readings you again would be forced to try to remember all the facts, dates, places, names, formulas, etc. that are required. The best memory in the world could not begin to do this feat. Since you could not re-listen to the lectures, that information would be lost or limited to your memory, which would be little at best. As for the text and assigned readings, you could reread them all or read what you had checked again. This would be a daunting task since you may have had to read several texts and several assigned reading books, not to mention web sites, videos, recordings etc. How could you possibly put all this information onto several pieces of paper that you could use as a master study list prior to tests or exams? YOU COULD NOT. IT IS THAT SIMPLE.

Let's assume that you have taken good notes for all the lectures you have attended and for all the important points made in texts and assigned readings.

Following good note-taking procedures, you have read over these notes every night and reviewed them all frequently.

THIS IS WHERE REAL LEARNING TAKES PLACE. THE CLASSROOM IS FOR OBTAINING INFORMATION; THE TAKING AND REREADING OF YOUR GOOD NOTES IS WHERE LEARNING TAKES PLACE.

Take your notes in a spiral notebook. Later, at your study place, put them in order under the subject you are learning in a large 3-ring binder. This binder never leaves your study place. The actual taking of notes is in itself part of the learning process, as is the rereading of them because when you write it "you can see it."

When it comes time to prepare for a test or final exam, completely review all your notes for the subject you are being tested on. Then make up a two-page single spaced MASTER STUDY LIST. This list contains all the major points, formulas, names, dates, times, places, etc. that are required to prepare for this test or exam. Study this list again and again just prior to the exam.

Isn't this a much more efficient and better way to prepare yourself for any testing situation?

SO YOU SEE, THE TAKING OF PROPER
NOTES IS NOT ONLY AN IMPORTANT
PART OF THE LEARNING PROCESS ITSELF,
IT ALLOWS YOU TO BECOME YOUR OWN
BEST TEACHER.

IF NOTE-TAKING WERE NOT THE MOST
EFFICIENT AND BEST WAY TO LEARN,
STUDY AND PREPARE FOR TESTING,
THEN WHY HAVE MILLIONS OF STUDENTS
ACROSS THE WORLD, FOR HUNDREDS OF
YEARS, ADOPTED IT IN ORDER
TO BECOME EXCELLENT STUDENTS?
IT'S YOUR CHOICE.

22
Basic Note-Taking

THIS IS THE MOST IMPORTANT SECTION OF THIS BOOK, because note-taking is the cornerstone for learning, studying, preparing to take tests and taking tests.

Taking notes and maintaining them is the most critical part of learning. It does not matter if you are in intermediate, high school, college or graduate school. The ability to take and maintain proper notes from lectures and reading materials is the main way to learn and succeed with excellent grades. With that said, let's take a look at what you have to do in order to take and maintain notes.

The first thing you need to do is buy yourself some inexpensive wire bound 3-ring notebooks that are college ruled. They usually have seventy pages, but sometimes more. The second thing you are going to do is take a ruler and draw a vertical line about 3 inches in from the wire binder. This leaves you with two columns, one on the left that is about 3 inches wide and one on the right that is about 5½ inches wide.

Take notes from lectures using the space on the right, and notes from your texts and reading assignments on the one on the left. Hopefully the notes taken from the text and reading assignments will support the notes on the right taken from your lecture. <u>Print on every other line</u>. This is so that when you are going over your notes each night after class you can add or delete information to your notes. THIS IS A MUST!

One of the many advantages of using these inexpensive wire notebooks is that you no longer have to carry a large, cumbersome, heavy 3-ring binder to class every day. If a text or other instructional materials are not needed for class work that given day, all you need to carry around are the notebook and two pens. Why two pens? What are you going to do if one runs out of ink? You need a spare.

Each night when you tear out the notes you have taken that day, insert them into a 2" thick 3-ring binder that has dividers for each subject you are taking. **THIS 3-RING BINDER NEVER LEAVES THE HOUSE.** You do not take it to school because if you were to lose all your notes for the entire semester for all your courses, **YOU WOULD BE DOOMED WHEN IT COMES TIME TO STUDY AND PREPARE FOR FINAL EXAMS.**

Take the wire-bound subject notebook to class to take notes and then transfer them that night to your 3-ring binder. You could live with it if you lost your notebook with the day's notes in it, but not the whole collection of notes for all your courses that you have kept safely at home.

This planned system of taking and maintaining notes has been used successfully by millions of students for many ears. As you progress in your education you may wish to adopt a different more involved system. This is fine, but for now follow the KISS formula. (KISS stands for "Keep It Simple, Stupid.")

22
Lecture Or Classroom Note-Taking

To most of you, note-taking is a new experience and you do not have a clue as to what to take notes on in class or from your texts or reading assignments. The purpose here is to take notes on the main ideas being presented. How do you determine what the main ideas are? There are some simple guidelines to follow, and I have listed them for you:

1. Always put the name of the course and date at the top of the page. This makes filing easy.

2. There is always some main topic being covered for that lecture or reading assignment. Give your notes a heading with this topic.

3. Teachers and textbook writers have always given students clues as to what is important for you to know, and therefore what is important to note. Here is a listing of what most teachers say or do to alert you to an important point:

"I can not stress this point enough"
"To sum up"
"In conclusion"
"Therefore"
"This is a critical point"
"In review"
"Last class we covered"
"Today we are going to cover"

4. The beginning and end of a lecture are the two most important parts to it, because most teachers will review the previous lecture at the beginning and review the present one at the end.

THIS IS THE TIME WHEN YOU HAVE TO FOCUS ON LISTENING.

5. Your biggest problem in note-taking is not the note-taking itself, it is staying alert and not letting your mind wander during the lecture, no matter how boring.

Things you can do to avoid this:

► Get to class early so you can get a good seat.

► Do not go to a lecture hungry.

► Do not eat a large meal just before a lecture.

► Do not sit next to someone who is going to be a distraction.

► Take notes. It helps you stay awake in a boring class.

► Sit up front. By doing so you do away with some distractions, have a better view of the chalkboard, hear better and stay more alert since you are so close to the teacher.

► Always be polite to classmates and the teacher. ALWAYS.

► Get a good night's sleep prior to the lecture.

► ABOVE ALL, ALWAYS AND I MEAN ALWAYS LOOK INTERESTED. NOTE-TAKING IS ABSOLUTELY THE MAIN, BEST AND SHORTEST WAY STUDENTS LEARN.

Like it or not, you had better get used to this fact and adapt to it, because note-taking is going to be the main way you are not only going to learn, but to study and prepare to take tests and exams. Why? Every study done, every book on learning and every good student can attest to the fact that taking good notes and maintaining them is an absolute must if you are going to succeed at this educational game. Properly-taken notes reviewed each night after class or after a text study session will provide you with a simple and easy way to track your learning AND DO IT CORRECTLY IN THE SHORTEST AMOUNT OF TIME.

In other words, when done properly your notes from class lectures plus test reviews provide you with a proven road map to your studies. That's why it is so important to take them correctly and maintain them during the semester. Then you can rely on them to be your main source of information for learning subject material, and to prepare you to pass quizzes, tests and exams.

23
Outside Of Classroom Note-Taking

Taking notes from reading is different from taking notes from class or lectures. It requires a greater amount of concentration. It requires more active intelligence and constant questioning. Your main goal is to record the major points in the reading. You need to think critically and interact with what you read.

Under the section on Reading Texts and Assigned Reading, we go over how to skim-read a chapter. During this skim read, ask yourself questions such as: *Why am I reading this? What am I supposed to learn from it?* Put these questions in your notes as you read, and when you complete the reading a little bit later, see if that reading gives you the answers. The object here is to keep your mind on the material being read, so that your mind does not wander. Just reading and really not knowing what you have read is like not reading it at all, so do it right the first time and you will not have to reread the chapter again.

As you read you need to be aware of just what you should be taking notes on. Try to become a critical reader and try your best to keep ahead of the author.

Some of the main things you want to keep in mind while reading are as follows:

1. Does the author discuss the pros and cons of the material?

2. Are lists of names, places, happenings, etc., important?

3. Are the causes and effects of something worth noting?

4. Are there rules and exceptions?

24
Tips On Taking Good Notes

1. Keep your notes short and simple.

2. Zero in on new information.

3. Note names, dates, places, theories and concepts.

4. Forget spelling and grammar.

5. Keep the big picture in focus.

6. Even if you are in the dark about what is being said, keep printing.

7. Remember, these are your personal notes. Nobody else is going to read them.

8. Avoid complete sentences.

9. Sum up long-winded presentations with a few key words.

10. Use abbreviations whenever possible. Check out the list of them provided earlier in this book.

11. Use signs and symbols you already know.

25
The Cornell
Note-Taking Method

The note-taking method covered in this book is a simplified version of the Cornell method, which is the most popular method available. This method provides a systematic format for condensing and organizing notes without laborious recopying.

After writing notes in the main column, use the left-hand column to label each idea and detail with a key word or "cue." (Go to your internet search engine and type in "The Cornell Note-Taking Method.")

26
Reading Over Your Notes

Ask yourself questions. Questions like:

"What is this author or lecturer trying to teach me?"

"How does this information fit into the total scope of the course?"

"Do I really have a good grasp of the information being presented?"

It is always a good idea to meet with a fellow classmate to share your notes. Make sure you pick someone who has taken good notes. You have heard the expression "Two heads are better than one." This may or may not be the case here, but sharing a note-comparing session with a classmate is a small but wonderful study session.

Remember when I told you not to underline or highlight the books or texts you read? Now I am telling you to do just that with regard to your notes. Pick the highlight color of your choice. When reading over your notes, highlight every single main point in them for that day.

Remember when I was listing the number of note pages you could end up with at the end of a semester? If you just take one page of notes per day per subject (and there are 96 days of instruction in a semester), that means you will have 96 pages of notes to go over for your final exam in each subject, and you have five times this much to review because you are taking five courses. So what you do is highlight the main points for each day's notes and when it comes time to make up your master two-page, single-spaced study list, you will be able to do this task rather easily. If I had only known this method when I was back in school, life would have been soooo much sweeter…and easier!

There are also excellent internet sites pertaining to note-taking. I urge you to check them out, since I can not present all there is to know on this subject in this book.

27
Listening For Content

I know, I know. You are probably saying, "I already know how to listen, so why are we taking it up now?" We are taking it up now because the majority of students are poor listeners, as judged by many experts and teachers. Listening for normal conversation is one thing; listening for subject content that you wish to remember is another.

If a special event you consider very important in your life happens, you can remember years later the exact details of that event. Why? Because you unconsciously told your brain to remember it. In listening for remembering subject material in your studies, you have to develop the listening skills that will tell your brain to remember. Listening like this *is* a skill and can be developed.

Here is how:

▶ To be a motivated listener, you have to consider the person talking worth listening to.

▶ It is your job to try your best to understand speakers, not theirs to help you.

► Do away with any distractions that will pull your attention from the speaker. Always take good notes of the speaker's main points; this will help you remember the speech later. It is natural for your mind to wander, especially when listening to a dull speech. If the speech is important enough for you to listen to, then do your best to keep your mind from wandering and keep tuned in to the speech. Try to determine where the speaker is going. By having an idea of where the speech is going, it will help keep your attention and give you a better idea of how it will develop. It is also natural to tune out someone that has some sort of distracting mannerism or dress that distracts you from what is being said. You are there to learn something, so ignore these distractions, and pay attention to the content of the speech.

► When talking to students about this subject, use a phrase that you might want to remember. Students that are good listeners should be focusing on actively listening for subject content. So the next time you hear a lecture, try to remember this, and definitely FOCUS ON LISTENING.

28
Your Grade Point Average (GPA)

The only way you can keep track of how you are doing in school or college is by monitoring your GPA after each grading period. If you have any chance of attending the college or advanced training of your choice, you will need to earn a respectable GPA. Many students do not know how a GPA is computed, so here is a simple explanation.

Each letter grade
is given a numerical value:

A = 4 points
B = 3 points
C = 2 points
D = 1 point
F = 0 points

Normally in high school and college most students take four or five courses each semester or quarter. Let's say you get the following grades in the courses listed:

English	B	=	3 points
Math	C	=	2 points
History	A	=	4 points
Social Studies	B	=	3 points
Science	B	=	3 points
Total points earned			15 points

15 divided by number of courses taken (5) gives you a GPA of 3.0

29
Your Brain

In a book like this we cannot go into an in-depth discussion of the brain, but we can list the most important facts about it as they relate to you as a student.

1. The brain is two sided: left for logical reasoning and analysis, and right for creativity and intuition.

2. There are three learning functions: visual, auditory and kinesthetic.

3. There are over one hundred billion neurons in the brain, and they continue to increase no matter what age you are.

4. Expert opinion varies, but on average we only use 5% of our brain's capacity, so no more "tired brain" excuses.

5. The brain gives a person the capacity to become a genius.

Do not expect your brain to immediately remember all the facts and ideas you have stored in it. Give it a few minutes to work on what you are asking it to do, especially in tough situations.

Have you ever tried to remember something and just couldn't do it right away, but after a few minutes of rest you came up with the answer? Keep this thought in mind when taking tests. If you don't know the answer to a question, mark it with a check next to the number and return to it later. Many times your brain will remember what it could not earlier, and then you can go back and answer the checked questions.

Sometimes other questions in a test will give you the answer to the earlier question, or trigger your brain to come up with the correct answer.

IMPORTANT: REMEMBER TO LEAVE YOURSELF ENOUGH TIME NEAR THE END OF THE TEST TO GO BACK OVER THE QUESTIONS YOU HAVE CHECKED.

30
Remembering

Mnemonic Devices

Your brain is like a large computer, but so much is stored there it is difficult to recall specific things on a moment's notice. Experts have determined that it helps if you can come up with some sort of "trigger" that will enable you to remember things. The following is one of the most common ones used:

Thirty days hath September, April, June and November.
All the rest have thirty one, except February, which has 28.

You can make up your own rhymes to help you remember anything. Remembering a story or an incident or happening can help you remember specific facts about something.

Acronyms

An acronym is a word formed by taking the first letters from several words in a series such as the popular SCUBA - S (self) C (contained) U (underwater) B (breathing) A (apparatus). Acronyms can be helpful in assisting you to remember a long list of things, especially if you have to remember them in order. You can make up your own acronym to help you remember anything.

Reminder Lists

I have found that one of the things I do to help me remember things is to make a list of them and pin it up above my desk. Every time I look up, there is a list, and I take a quick look at it and then remember why I put it there. I am a great believer in making out "To Do" lists. In this fast-moving, ever- changing society of ours, it is impossible to remember all the many things we have to do both at work and at home, so I make up "To Do" lists for both.

You can attack these lists in a number of ways. Take them in the order you put them down. Do the most difficult ones first. Do the easiest ones first. You get the idea. Me, I complete the easiest ones first, thereby making my list shorter quickly, and I get satisfaction at completing so many so quickly. My wife loves this approach because I get a lot of her "Honey Do" projects completed quickly.

As a student, you should complete the tasks on your list that are due the earliest, thereby giving you time to do the others at a slower pace. This is a very individual thing, so adopt the way that works the best for you.

31
How To Do Your Best On Any Type Of Test

1. READ ALL THE TEST DIRECTIONS CAREFULLY. MANY STUDENTS HAVE FAILED A TEST JUST BECAUSE THEY DID NOT READ OR FOLLOW THE INSTRUCTIONS.

2. Decide whether to go quickly or slowly.

3. Budget your time for each section of the test.

4. Take the easy questions first, mark the ones you do not know and return to them later.

5. Read all the essay questions in advance and if you're allowed, choose the one you know the most about to write on.

6. Leave questions that will take up a lot of time until later and move on.

7. Check your watch or the clock at sensible intervals.

8. Use all the time allowed. If you finish early, go back over the test for accuracy.

WATCH OUT FOR CARELESS ERRORS AND DOUBLE CHECK YOUR ANSWERS AT THE END OF THE TEST

1. Reread all questions if you have time. You might have missed something or a later question might have triggered a different response, or your brain might have kicked into gear.

2. Are all your numbers legible?

3. Have you filled in the correct blanks?

REASONING OUT TOUGH QUESTIONS

1. Look for clues in the question.

2. Look for clues in the answer choices.

3. Keep your mind open for memory joggers.

4. Save tough questions for last.

5. Do not assume there are hidden meanings on teacher-prepared tests.

32
Pre-Test Study Strategies

The first thing you need to find out is what kind of test is going to be given. Most instructors will gladly tell you if you ask them.

If the test is going to be a short answer, fill-in-the blank, matching, or true-false, you need to learn specific facts and details.

If the test is going to be an essay test, you will need knowledge to argue persuasively about several general topics and back up your arguments with thoughtful responses.

IF POSSIBLE, REVIEW PAST EXAMS GIVEN BY THE INSTRUCTOR. MANY INSTRUCTORS WILL PROVIDE THESE WHEN ASKED.

Ask yourself the following questions:

1. Is the teacher after straight memorization?

2. Did former tests focus on trivia or on major principles?

3. Were the questions abstract or concrete?

4. Did the teacher's lectures favor facts or ideas?

5. How were tests scored?

6. Were there trick questions?

FROM YOUR CLASSROOM EXPERIENCE, WHAT DID THE INSTRUCTOR PAY THE MOST ATTENTION TO?

1. What did the instructor emphasize most frequently?

2. Did he/she focus on assignments?

3. Which topics were singled out or stressed?

4. Were tricky questions used?

5. What is the teacher's goal or attitude?

33
Preparing For Quizzes, Tests And Exams

1. Practice test-taking by making up your own exams from past assignments and from test questions at the back of each chapter in your text.

2. Try to set up, as closely as you can, an actual test situation.

3. Set time limits on yourself while pre-testing.

PREPARE EXTRA FOR PROBLEM-SOLVING AND ESSAYS.

1. Choose 8-10 subject-oriented essay questions to practice.

2. Outline your practice essays following the major points listed in the Essay Checklist covered in this book on page 115.

34
Scheduling And Preparing For Tests And Exams

BEFORE YOU BEGIN STUDYING

~ Get test information.

~ Try finding like-minded classmates with whom to study.

A WEEK BEFORE THE EXAM

~ Read through all the notes you have for that subject.

~ Create a two-page master study list from the notes you took in class and from the readings. Pay particular attention to key words, themes and concepts.

~ Meet with your study group.

FIVE DAYS BEFORE THE EXAM

~ Study your master list.

~ Use flash cards to help you go over key words, places and facts.

~ Take notes on main ideas, anticipating possible essay questions/answers.

~ Schedule time to talk with your instructor if there is still information that you are unsure of.

~ Meet with your study group and read through all reference materials.

THE NIGHT BEFORE THE EXAM

~ Do one final read-through of your master lists and go through flash cards.

~ Go over possible essay questions and answers.

~ Create a list of hard-to-remember terms.

~ Organize materials needed for exam: books, pens, list, and anything else you might need for the test.

~ Relax and get a full night's sleep.

THE DAY OF THE EXAM

~ Mentally go over key terms and ideas.

~ Eat a light breakfast.

~ If you have time, do one final read-through of your master study list.

~ Bring all your materials.

~ Get to class early to get a good seat.

~ Go into the test with a positive outlook.

~ Dress comfortably, but dress as if you expect to succeed.

~ Know your rights as a student. If you feel ill or become ill, don't try to tough it out and take the test. You have the right to ask for a postponement, so do so.

~ Do not forget to use the "Brain Drain" prior to starting the actual exam. (This is explained later in this book.)

This is a suggested schedule that can be modified to fit your needs.

35
How To Avoid Stress

1. Keep up with your daily assignments. Once you fall behind it is difficult to catch up.

2. Review your notes daily and highlight the main points.

3. Make plans for whatever you have to do and set up a schedule.

4. Don't be a hero and take on more than you can handle.

5. Do your best; even if you know it's not great, it should be the best that you can do.

6. There comes a time when EVERYONE NEEDS SOME EXTRA HELP. Do not be ashamed to ask. You might ask a classmate, a teacher, go to the library, tutorial center or go on line, whatever. It is much better to recognize you need help and get it rather than fail.

Do not try to become a workaholic in your studying. Take time to rest your mind and take some breaks. When you return to your studies you will find that you are more relaxed and able to do a better job.

Keeping Up Your Health

1. Eat healthy meals on a regular basis.

2. Stay away from sick people.

3. Get enough restful sleep.

4. Wash your hands thoroughly before eating anything.

5. Exercise regularly.

6. Dress properly for the weather.

7. Keep your fingers out of your mouth and nose; that's how germs invade your body.

Worry

1. "Self-fulfilling prophesy" is a tendency to do as well, or as poorly as expected. In other words, go into the test with positive thoughts, not negative ones.

2. Dress accordingly. You want to dress so you are comfortable, but at the same time you want to feel confident, and if that means wearing some of your better clothes to the test, DO IT.

3. Get yourself in a good mood. Avoid depressing situations and seek out enjoyable ones.

4. Rid yourself of any anger or negative thoughts.

5. If you actually become terrorized by the testing experience, you owe it to yourself and your parents to ask for and obtain professional counseling to help you overcome this problem. Test anxiety is a common problem for many students and there are special solutions if you obtain expert help.

36
Learning Math

For many students, math is the most difficult subject to master. Here are a few ideas that might help you:

1. The following is probably the most important point under this heading and that is why it is in all caps and bold.

DO REQUIRED HOMEWORK ON A REGULAR BASIS. MATH IS A BUILDING PROCESS AND IN ORDER TO UNDER-STAND THE NEXT STEP, YOU NEED TO KNOW THE PRESENT AND PREVIOUS STEPS.

IT IS A LOT EASIER TO LEARN MATH THIS WAY THAN LEARNING IT ON YOUR OWN OUT OF THE TEXT.

2. Keep paying attention in class. Every minute you daydream will cost you that many more minutes of studying later.

3. Try to get copies of old tests your teacher has given and study them.

4. Set up test-taking situations. Make up your own test from unanswered text questions, and set time limits on yourself.

5. Set up a study group with a few dedicated friends. You can help each other. Help fellow group members by teaching them the material. If you can't teach it, you do not know it!

37
Strategies For Learning

True/False Tests

1. To be true, the entire statement must be true. If a part is true and a part is false, the entire item is false.

2. Watch out for absolutes and qualifiers. "Always," "never," "all" and "none" are often incorrect.

3. Words such as "usually," "sometimes" and "generally" are often found in true statements, but they might also be found in false statements.

4. Make sure you know all your vocabulary.

5. Look for key words to determine the meaning of a statement. One word can make an otherwise true statement false.

6. Read each item with care and make sure you understand what the sentence means.

7. If you don't know the answer to a question, it's wise to skip that question and return to it later.

Multiple Choice Tests

Multiple choice tests are the most popular with teachers and national testing agencies. The reason is that they are quick and easy to score and can be reused in a different order and manner later on. They can also be easily adapted to almost any subject.

YOU HAVE TO REMEMBER THEY ARE NOTHING BUT AN ELIMINATION CONTEST. YOU HAVE TO ELIMINATE THE ANSWERS THAT ARE THE LEAST CORRECT AND PICK THE ANSWER THAT IS THE MOST CORRECT. TO DO SO, THINK OF THE FOLLOWING:

1. Again, follow all instructions to the letter.

2. How many of the responses make sense? Discard the ones that do not, zero in on the ones that do and then choose the most correct answer.

3. There is probably one clue word that makes one response better than the others.

4. Eliminate implausible answers.

5. Watch out for absolutes and qualifiers. "Always," "never," "all" and "none" are often incorrect.

6. Be sure you read all responses; the first one may be correct, but a later response may be more correct.

7. The greater the numbers of ridiculous choices you eliminate, the better your odds are of choosing the correct answer.

8. Look for familiar phrases or questions right out of your textbook.

9. Toward the end of the test period go back and check your flagged questions and then answer them as well as you can.

10. Reread all your answers if you have the time. Make sure your name is at the top of the test.

Matching Tests

1. Make sure you read all the directions.

2. Match the easy ones first.

3. Work through the longer phrases next.

Short Answer, Completion and Fill-In-The-Blank Tests

1. Look for clues.

2. Don't over-think the questions.

3. If you can't decide between two answers, use both. It's better to over-answer than not answer at all.

4. Make educated guesses.

Vocabulary Tests

1. Beware of words that are too similar to the correct answer.

2. Pay attention to grammar and spelling.

3. Eliminate incorrect speech.

4. Don't leave blanks – guess.

Number Problem Tests

1. Make sure you work carefully and precisely.

2. If you can, use a calculator to check your work.

3. Use all information. Study all the graphs and charts thoroughly.

4. Reread the question frequently.

Essay Tests

1. Read through all the questions. Make a list for each one of everything you know about that question. This will jog your memory.

2. Underline key words and re-read the directions.

3. Keep track of your time.

4. Make an outline prior to writing.

5. Organize your essay, using a topic sentence, support paragraphs and a conclusion.

EVEN IF YOU'VE MISTAKENLY PREPARED FOR THE WRONG TOPICS, WRITE WHAT YOU KNOW TO GET PARTIAL CREDIT.

Essay Checklist

1. Is there a clear and concise thesis and topic?

2. Have I thoroughly proven my topic and thesis?

3. Is each paragraph clearly related to the topic?

4. Does each paragraph have a central theme or idea?

5. Has each idea been comprehensively proven and argued?

6. Are there clear transitions from one paragraph to the next? Do the paragraphs follow logically?

7. Have I made sure that each sentence and idea is relevant to the topic?

8. Does the paper as a whole make sense? Have all words been used correctly?

9. Have I checked grammar, spelling and punctuation?

10. If I used quotes or examples, are they used in the proper manner?

Numbers 11-14 pertain to out-of-class assignments.

11. Have I used a thesaurus and dictionary in the final proofing of my writing?

12. Is my bibliography in the correct format?

13. Is my paper double-spaced and stapled together? Is my name and page number on each page and have I included a cover sheet complete with my name, course title and date?

14. Do I have an extra copy?

38
What To Do
In The Testing Room

1. Tests are a necessary part of life, and not just in education. So rather than fight them, accept them for what they are, and try to do your best with them.

2. Get to the test room early so you can get settled and relaxed.

3. Concentrate and block out all distractions.

4. Sit away from windows, aisles and friends.

5. Sit near good lighting.

6. Close door if noisy or drafty.

7. Bring necessary supplies and a snack.

8. Bring sweater if necessary.

9. Bring a watch to pace yourself.

DON'T LET TEST-TAKING ANXIETY GET YOU DOWN...BEING ANXIOUS IS NORMAL.

39
Guessing

Depending on the type of test you are taking, the odds for guessing are as follows:

1. True/False: 50%/50%

2. Multiple Choice: With four answers 25% with five answers 20%.

3. Matching: Odds depend on the number of matches you have to make.

4. Number Problems: You have it or you don't, but if you show all your calculations you may get partial credit.

5. Essay: Write what you can on the topic. You may get partial credit.

6. Fill-in-the-blanks: You have it or you don't. Give it a try.

With this said, you should only guess at the end of the test when your brain has had a chance to take in all the information provided by absorbing all the test questions and answers, and you still have absolutely no clue what the right answer is.

THEN AND ONLY THEN SHOULD YOU RESORT TO GIVING IT YOUR BEST GUESS.

40
The Brain Drain

Right up until the time you entered the testing room, you should have been going over your Master Study List for this test. You can take it with you into the testing room and continue reading it there until the instructor tells everyone to put all books and papers under your desk. Once the exam is handed out, you should take the opportunity to jot down all the major facts (dates, places, ideas, names, etc.) you might need for the test on the back or on the margins of the test paper.

You have just left your Master Study List a few minutes ago, so your memory will never be fresher. This is a perfectly legal and ethical thing to do and cannot be considered cheating in any way. After all, you have only taken your memory into the testing room, not a crib sheet. This will only take a minute or so and might come in very handy later on in the test.

THIS ONE SIMPLE TESTING STRATEGY WOULD HAVE HELPED ME IN MANY HIGH SCHOOL AND COLLEGE EXAMS IF I HAD ONLY KNOWN. NOW YOU DO.

41
Choosing
A Cramming Method

Intense cramming a few days prior to the exam is not a good idea. It will create a lot of anxiety and poorly prepare you for most testing situations.

The best method of preparing is to follow the STUDY SCHEDULE CHECK LIST that was covered earlier. It will help you develop a schedule for preparing for tests. Be aware that you may have to adjust your schedule depending on the importance of the test.

Prepared cramming is done by going over your class and lecture notes and by making a two-page Master Study List that lists all the major topics covered in your notes for the period the test will cover. It is this Master Study List that you use right up to the time you enter the testing room. By having prepared properly and thoroughly, you then enjoy the following benefits:

1. Long-term memory

2. Less anxiety

3. Greater self-confidence

4. Condensed notes which contain all the main ideas and facts you need to know (vocabulary, formulas, dates, places, etc.)

5. A complete overview of the entire course

6. Facts in perspective

7. Feeling completely prepared

8. Most important – better performance

42
The Regular
High School Program

Ask some adults if they wish they had taken the forty courses that made up their high school program more seriously. The vast majority of them will say yes! Learn from their mistakes and try to do your absolute best. How well you do in those forty courses is a tremendous determiner on how well you will do with your future academic and professional life.

The regular high school program consists of forty courses. Each school district has its own requirments, but the following examples of a regular program and a college prep program are fairly typical. Normally, students take five courses per semester, for a total of ten per year. After four years, they will have completed forty courses.

The following is a typical four-year set of graduation requirements, followed by a schedule of classes for a regular high school diploma. You will notice that there are times when you will be able to select "elective" courses. Many students end their educational career by completing only the required high school program.

THIS COULD BE THE WORST MISTAKE YOU WILL MAKE IN YOUR ENTIRE LIFE.

The reason I say that is because if you later want to enroll in a college or some other advanced type of training that requires completion of a college prep program, you will not be able to do so.

You can complete those missing courses at an adult school or a community college later, but probably you will be working full-time and perhaps be raising a family. These responsibilities will make it very difficult for you to complete the four or five missing courses you <u>could</u> have and <u>should</u> have taken while in high school. So take those college-prep courses even if you have to get tutors to help you through them.

43
Graduation Requirements

The following are California-based requirements but are typical of most state requirements.

Students need to have a four-year educational plan to help them succeed in high school. Noted below are the credits, courses and standardized tests needed to graduate from high school. (The next section also describes a typical program for a college prep student.) You are encouraged to discuss your ideas with your parents, your teachers and your counselor, who will help you complete your four year educational plan.

1. UNITS OF CREDIT: 240 credits are required for graduation. Ten credits are earned for a passing grade of D or better in a year-long course.

2. COURSE REQUIREMENTS:

4 years . . . . English
1 year . . . . World History/Geography
   (May be taken in grade 9 or 10)
1 year . . . . United States History
1 year . . . . United States Government/Economics
1 year . . . . Biological Science
1 year . . . . Physical Science
2 years . . . . Mathematics (including Algebra I)
2 years . . . . . Foreign Language, Fine Arts, Career Tech
2 years . . . . .Physical Education

3. **COMPETENCY:** Students must achieve competency in MATHEMATICS and LANGUAGE ARTS by achieving a passing score on the High School Exit Exam.

COURSE SELECTION: Selection of courses should be based on the following criteria: (1) Past Achievement, (2) Test scores, (3) Teacher recommendations, (4) College entrance requirements, (5) Individual interest, (6) Career goals, and (7) Balanced program.

Your first goal is to earn a high school diploma.
You do this by earning <u>credits</u> in specific courses.

REGULAR FOUR-YEAR HIGH SCHOOL PLAN				
GRADE 9	**GRADE 10**	**GRADE 11**	**GRADE 12**	**Total Credits**
English 1	English 2	English 3	English 4	40 credits
World History/ Geography May be taken in grade 10		US History	US Gov. 1 semester Economics 1 semester	30 credits
PE	PE			20 credits
Math Algebra I must be taken/passed in intermediate or high school	Math			20 credits
	Biology	Physical Science		20 credits
FL/VPA/ TechEd	FL/VPA/ TechEd			20 credits
Electives	Electives	Electives	Electives	90+ credits
Total: **60-70 credits**	**Total:** **60-70 credits**	**Total:** **60-70 credits**	**Total:** **60-70 credits**	**Total Credits:** **≥ 240**

44
The College Prep High School Program

As stated earlier, each school district has different graduation requirements for its regular program and for its college-prep program. The main point to remember is that almost all of them require about five additional required courses beyond the regular program to complete the college-prep program – usually three years of a foreign language, Geometry and Algebra II.

I know what you're thinking, "The students that go on and take the college prep program are the brainy people, and I am just not that smart."

There is a way for you to master these five additional courses if you really are willing to make the effort. You will probably need some extra help in order to complete these five courses, but help is available in different ways.

Many schools now have free learning centers that provide extra tutorial help. Many schools also provide a list of advanced students who are willing to tutor for a minimal fee. There are all kinds of private tutorial programs available, but they are rather costly. The cheapest and probably best way to get help is to form a study group of fellow students and help each other.

You should not feel bad about seeking and obtaining tutorial help. The best athletes in the world have a number of professional tutors they pay thousands of dollars a day to help them. They are called coaches, but in reality they are just tutors.

If you would like to meet the subject requirements for a four-year college, you must take the following *minimum* subjects and earn high grades.

Many colleges require more than this minimum.

COLLEGE PREP FOUR-YEAR HIGH SCHOOL PLAN

GRADE 9	GRADE 10	GRADE 11	GRADE 12	Total Credits
English 1	English 2	English 3	English 4	40 credits
World History/ Geography May be taken in grade 10		US History	US Gov. 1 semester Economics 1 semester	30 credits
PE	PE			20 credits
Math (Algebra I)	Math (Geometry)	Math (Algebra II)	Math (opt)	20 credits
	Biology	Physical Science	Science (opt)	20 credits
For Language	For Language	For Language	For Lang (opt)	20 credits
At least 1 Visual/Performing Arts course taken during grade 9-12				10 credits
Electives	Electives	Electives	Electives	80+ credits
Total: 60-70 credits	**Total: 60-70 credits**	**Total: 60-70 credits**	**Total: 60-70 credits**	**Total Credits: ≥ 240**

45

Four Year Educational Planning Worksheet

9th Grade	CR
ENGLISH	
WORLD HISTORY/GEOG.	
MATH	
P.E.	
ELECTIVE	
ELECTIVE	
TOTAL	

Summer School

10th Grade	CR
ENGLISH	
MATH	
P.E.	
BIOLOGY	
ELECTIVE	
ELECTIVE	
TOTAL	

Summer School

11th Grade	CR
ENGLISH	
U.S. HISTORY	
PHYSICAL SCIENCE	
MATH	
ELECTIVE	
ELECTIVE	
TOTAL	

Summer School

12th Grade	CR
ENGLISH	
GOVT/ ECONOMICS	
ELECTIVE	
ELECTIVE	
ELECTIVE	
ELECTIVE	
TOTAL	

Summer School

131

Credit for Grad	CR
9th Grade	
10th Grade	
11th Grade	
12th Grade	
Summer School	
TOTAL	

College/Career Plans

46
Measuring And Monitoring Student Progress

With the adoption and maintenance of an organized note-taking system as outlined earlier in this book, parents now have the tools and techniques to measure and monitor progress. Students should be required to keep these notes in a stay-at-home three-ring binder, organized by subjects. They should also be required to keep copies of all completed and graded quizzes, tests and reports.

Parents need only request a review session with the student, preferably once a week, to go over these course materials. It is this weekly review that is critical to keep track of just how well students are doing with their studies. Most school terms are eighteen weeks long. This gives you eighteen review sessions to help guide students with their studies and determine if they need tutoring, which is covered earlier in this book.

THE END OF THE SCHOOL TERM (WHEN GRADES ARE AWARDED) IS NOT THE TIME TO DISCUSS GRADE PERFORMANCE.

Many states, like California, have implemented a Student Information System in nearly all school districts. This system allows both parents and students the opportunity to check on daily progress. A few clicks on a computer mouse and you can determine the up-to-date academic information on a student for each class, including current grades and assignments. It would be an excellent idea to check to see if your school district has such a Student Information System in operation. If they do, you can then learn how to access it.

47
Final Advice

It takes more than just wanting, wishing and hoping to become a success at anything. You have to pay your dues if you really want to succeed. Paying your dues in the academic world involves following time-proven organization, learning, studying, pre-testing and testing skills.

This book has made a modest attempt to provide you with the information needed to understand what is involved in each of these skills. It is up to you whether to utilize them or not. As a final reminder, here are the major points covered in this book:

1. Get yourself and your study place organized with the proper supplies.

2. Determine your learning styles using the learning strategies listed for your learning style. Check out the other strategies as well.

3. Try your best to follow the directions for taking, recording, maintaining and studying your class, text and reading notes. You must stick with this for an entire semester or quarter.

4. Try to adopt the many study strategies outlined.

5. Pay attention to the pre-testing and testing sections and use this information to do a better job in your testing experiences.

6. Give this an honest try, and I can practically guarantee that your grades will improve dramatically.

I know from many years of experience with both high school and college students that most of you will only adopt some of the various strategies covered in this book. You will pick and choose the ones that would be easiest to adopt and give them a half-hearted try. This would be the biggest mistake of your academic life.

Take what has been presented in this book to heart. It has taken years for you to get where you are grade wise, and it will take some time to change that. All I ask is that you give it an honest full semester or quarter, and you will see a major change in your grades.

Remember that working harder is not always the best way . . . working smarter is, and I sincerely hope that this book has taught you that.

Gary Edison Howard

Web Sites That Can Help You

1. Study Guides and Strategies: www.studygs.net
This site is the most comprehensive educational learning site I have found. The following main headings have many sub-headings that give detailed, easy-to-understand information on each topic listed.

Preparing	Classroom Participation	Writing Basics
Learning	Learning with Others	Writing Types
Studying	Online Learning/	Vocabulary/Spelling
Resources	Communications	Project Management
Research	Preparing for Tests	Math
Reading Skills	Taking Tests	Science and Technology

2. Diablo Valley College Online – DVC Learning Style Survey For College: www.metamath.com/lsweb/dvclearn.htm
This is the web site for Diablo Valley College in Pleasant Hill, California. This wonderful web site developed by Catherine Jester and Suzanne Miller does an excellent job of helping you determine what your learning style is and then provides you with learning strategies for each style. The easy 32-question online test only takes a few minutes and gives you an excellent insight into which learning style is best for you.

3. Reference or Study Guides: www.quickstudy.com
This is the site for BarCharts Inc., probably the largest supplier of study guides in the U.S. Most guides cost from $3.95 to $5.95 each. Phone: 1-800-226-7799. E-mail: studyaid@barcharts.com

4. Procrastination: www.studygs.net/attmot3.htm
This web site provides you with useful tips to help build better work and study habits.

137

5. The Use of Index Cards: www.studygs.net/tstprp4.htm

This web site offers a one-page summary about how to use index cards to succeed in school.

6. Taking Notes In Class:
www.how-to-study.com/taking-notes-in-class.htm

This web site offers information about taking notes efficiently during class.

7. Acronyms: www.thememorypage.net/acro.htm

This web site offers a long list of useful acronyms.

8. Studying In A Group:
www.tcd.ie/Student_Counselling/docs/study_groups.pdf

This web site from Trinity College in Dublin explains group study in great detail. They also offer a list of guidelines for setting up your own study group.

9. Overcoming Test Stress: www.studygs.net/tstprp8.htm

This study web site offers worthwhile tips for preparing for a big test and dealing with anxiety.

10. Avoiding Plagiarism: www.umuc.edu/library/copy.html

This web site from the University of Maryland University College explains copyright and fair use policies for college students and faculty.

The Most Often Misspelled Words In English

a while
acceptable
accidentally
accommodate
accordion
acquire
acquit
all right
a lot
amateur
apparent
argument
atheist
believe
broccoli
business
calendar
camouflage
cantaloupe
Caribbean
category
cemetery
changeable
chili
collectible
colonel
column
committed
committee

conscience
conscientious
conscious
consensus
coolly
corroborate
counterfeit
daiquiri
dealt
definite(ly)
descendant
despair
dilemma
deterrence
disappoint
discipline
drunkenness
dumbbell
ecstasy
eighth
embarrass(ment)
equipment
exhilarate
exceed
existence
experience
fascinate
February
fiery

foreign
forty
fulfill
gauge
government
grammar
grateful
guarantee
handkerchief
harass
height
hierarchy
hoarse
holiday
humorous
hypocrisy
icicles
ignorance
imagine
imitate
immediate
incredible
independent
indispensable
innocent
inoculate
irresistible
irritable
intelligence

its/it's
jealousy
jewelry
just deserts
kernel
league
license
leisure
liaison
library
license
lightning
losing
maintenance
maneuver
marshmallow
medieval
memento
millennium
miniature
minuscule
mischievous
misogyny
missile
misspell
nauseous
neighbor
necessary
ninth
no one
noticeable
occasion
occasionally

occurrence
often
optimistic
pamphlet
parallel
pastime
peculiar
perseverance
persistent
personnel
phenomenon
pigeon
playwright
plenitude
possession
precede
principal/principle
privilege
procedure
pronunciation
publicly
pursuit
queue
questionnaire
raspberry
receive/receipt
recommend
referred
reference
relevant
repetition
restaurant
ridiculous

rhyme
rhythm
roommate
sandal
schedule
scissors
seize
separate
sergeant
sophomore
subtle
supersede
surgeon
their/they're/
there
threshold
tomorrow
tongue
tragedy
truly
turmeric
twelfth
tyranny
until
vacuum
vengeance
vicious
warrant
weather
weird
wholly
yacht
yield

HELP YOUR KIDS GET BETTER GRADES

ORDER FORM

Please send _____ copies at $11.95 each to:

Name _____

Address _____

City _____

State _____ Zip _____

Phone _____

E-mail _____

Sales Tax:
   Please add 9.25% for books sent to California address

Shipping:
   U.S. ~ $3.00 for first book, $1.00 each additional book
   Canada ~ $5.00 for first book, $3.00 each additional book

Send form to: Cambridge Learning Skills Publishing
1850 Joseph Drive, Moraga, CA 94556

To order by internet: www.WantBetterGrades.com

To order by E-mail: G.Howard@comcast.net

Quantity Discounts: Large discounts are available for quantity orders. Please see the internet site for a listing of the discounts we offer.

141

Proof

Made in the USA
Charleston, SC
24 June 2010